To Tyler

SIMMSBURGH
BY
PAUL NAYLOR

Best Wishes

Paul Naylor

ILLUSTRATED

BY

JOAN BRICKLEY

PREFACE

World war one was a devastating experience and so many people were hit hard. My mother sadly passed away in childbirth, when I was being born. My father, who is now the Duke of Waltonshire, was never the same after such a traumatic experience.

Although the family residence Simmsburgh Castle was functioning, it went into slow decline, When I became of age, I began the slow process of taking on the mantra. With my new wife Gertrude, we breathed new life into the old rugged castle.

CHAPTER ONE

During the 'roaring' 1920s, my family became

estranged from all their friends in London.

My father had sold the family business and

moved the family back, to live full time, at

Simmsburgh Castle. It was certainly large

enough for all the family, although the

younger ones, like myself, preferred London,

where all the nightlife was.

After I'd finished at university, my father

taught me all that was necessary for me to be

able to, eventually, take over the running of Simmsburgh Castle.

My father was the Duke of Waltonshire, and I his heir, next in line to inherit the title and castle.

He had made his fortune on the stock market but could see that the good times were coming to an end.

The family's wealth was transferred to the castle along with all the family possessions. Simmsburgh was one of the largest castles in the country; at one time, we used to have three estates, in different parts of the country. One estate, in London was sold to developers; the second, together with its manor house, was sold to a wealthy industrialist.

The family ended up keeping just the castle, with all it's one thousand and fifty two rooms, although it was in need of modernising in quite a few areas.

The castle itself was situated in twenty-five square miles of open land and the estate also owned many towns and villages in the surrounding area.

While I took charge of Simmsburgh Castle, my father remained in London, it was from there that he conducted his business, which was mainly attending at the House of Lords.

In 1928, when I reached a milestone, my twenty-first birthday, the process of my 'new' education began, that of my learning the etiquette and responsibilities of how to become the next Duke of Waltonshire.

It would take seven long years of sheer hard work.

I only had a father's hand to guide and encourage me, as sadly, my mother had died giving birth to me, a blow from which my father, to this day, has never really recovered.

By all accounts she was a wonderful woman, and for a while, after she had passed away, father lost all interest in the running and the upkeep of the estate.

Although the estate was still just about functioning, it had been neglected badly and allowed to run down over the years.

Therefore, as heir, it fell to me to update and modernise the castle, and somehow breathe new life into the estate. Fortunately for me, about this same time, I met a wonderful girl named Gertrude, with whom I fell in love and very quickly made my wife and embarked on a new life together. However, little did we know, as we began that new life, the problems, both big and small, we would have to deal with on the 'rocky road' called life.

My father was happiest in London with his close friends around him, but he did return to the castle every year during the House of Lords' Summer Recess. When he arrived he never lived in the castle itself. He very much preferred to stay in the old lodge on the edge of the castle grounds.

With all the plans and arrangements that had

to be made, it took almost twelve months for

Gertrude and I to settle happily into the castle

and call it home.

All the family members lived there with us.

They moved in from the other two estates that

had been sold and; all the generations, from

grandparents to grandchildren, from aunts

and uncles to nieces, nephews and cousins,

we accommodated them all. As the years went by, most of them either married, or moved to live on other parts of the Simmsburgh estate, but the castle itself remained the centre of attention for all major family events, and celebrations.

Some years before, my father had been unjustly and unfairly ousted from the family business, a business which the family had owned for at least three generations but those upstarts had had to be made to pay out a fortune in compensation and, most fortunately for us, they were never able to get their hands on either Simmsburgh Castle or any part of the Simmsburgh Estate.

Business can be a funny game. You never know what's just around the corner.

My father must have seen the trouble coming for some time as he always used to say that 'greed will get the best of them every time.'

Our family was fortunate in being able to hold on to our castle and estates, because we had a long, and fruitful history of experience.

CHAPTER TWO

My wife, Gertrude, and I settled into Simmsburgh Castle and made all the necessary plans for renovations and alterations. Gertrude was the third cousin of the Dowager of Stonehaven Manor. The Dowager had recently been widowed, and had taken over the manor, which was the protocol of the time.

The Dowager, being an American lady, was full of bright and unusual ideas, unlike British aristocrats, she ran the Manor House in a very businesslike way, although, in her heart, she loved Stonehaven Manor so much she made it into a warm, welcoming, family home. As our families were related, we used to spend time there, mainly at Easter, when we would stay over and enjoy the spring break. Following the Dowager's example, we decided to follow her ideas at Simmsburgh Castle. But it would take time to install everything that was needed. On reflection, it was to be a lifetime's work.

But after all, it was a way of life, not a job.

Being the glorious twenties, good staff were at a premium; many good men had been either killed or wounded in the Great War.

The country had recovered somewhat, but

thousands and thousands of men had been

lost in the conflict.

Simmsburgh Castle and the surrounding

estate were no different than anywhere else.

In the small township of Fernbourne, all the

men had been lost at the Battle of the

Somme. Other townships on the estate

suffered heavy losses too. The young boys

that had been left behind, not being old

enough to go to war, had now become men.

In time, they would marry and go on to have

children of their own, breathing much needed

new life into the surrounding townships and villages.

Having made all the plans for Simmsburgh Castle, I decided, for a little respite, to travel up to London. While there, I stayed in the family's townhouse with my father.

It was so good for us to be able to spend quality time together, something we were rarely able to do. While I was there, I showed him the plans that I had drawn up for the renovation and remodeling of the Castle. He scrutinised them in detail and although he approved in the main, he did make some minor alterations and additions of his own. Without the people of the townships and villages, the castle wouldn't be able to function. The castle and the people needed each other, one thrived off the other. With this in mind, the Simmington Co-operative Society was formed.

People in the townships and villages were enrolled and became full members. All profits made were divided equally between each member. These people, in time, would run every aspect of the Society, top to bottom, and a training programme was set in place from the very beginning.

Simmington Co-operative Society would own, and operate, a variety of trades, from shops, solicitors, funeral parlours, transport, construction, estate agents and even an employment agency, all helping to provide the workforce for the estate, covering every aspect needed to keep both the castle and estate running smoothly, efficiently and effectively.

Twenty five million pounds was set aside to launch the project. My father, himself, had agreed this amount, for it was something he was passionate about. My family loaned The Society the money, and it was agreed that it would be paid back, with interest, over an agreed period of time.

CHAPTER THREE

In the winter of 1928, my father and I decided

that we would spend time again, together, at

the London townhouse where we would not

be interrupted, while going over, and putting

into action plans for the castle, everything we

needed was also to be found in the city.

 For such a major project, we needed the best

people.

It would take time to set up such a major

project as this was, and it was good to be

working side by side with my father. The

townhouse was run by twelve servants. I had

my own separate apartments and personal

valet, George, brought from Simmsburgh.

During my younger years, whenever I was in

London, my room was always ready for me

and the house was also used by any member

of the family when we needed to meet or

discuss family affairs. The family's personal

solicitors were also based in London, and it

was there that all my own personal business

was conducted. He also made great use of

the townhouse when he had to attend the

House of Lords.

It was far less expensive than using hotels,

even though he had a ten percent stake in

The Royale Bettington Hotel, he still preferred

the townhouse.

The Royale Bettington was the family's main

source of income, it was a very high end,

most exclusive hotel with a casino, and

occupied a prime location.

My father's friend, the Duke of

Garswoodshire, was the main shareholder

owning ninety percent of the elegant place,

but, as my father had owned the land in the

first place, sold it, he then struck a deal.

When the hotel was completed our family

would receive a ten percent share of the company.

Although most aristocratic families had, more or less, recovered from the war, the roaring twenties would be, for a lot of these families, one last fling.

It was the 'Roaring Twenties' after all but, eventually, all good things come to an end, and in lots of people's cases, it would be sooner rather than later. My father and his small, but distinguished, circle of friends, such as the Duke of Garswoodshire, were convinced in their own minds, that the good times would soon be over.

They thought there would be a financial crash sooner rather than later.

But no one seemed to be taking heed of the warning signs all around them, many people continued living on credit, and that credit was fast running out, like a steam train at full speed.

While I was away in London, my wife Gertrude, took up the enormous challenge of reorganising the castle, with the help of our extended family, who were magnificent in their own ways, but the way in which we did things had become rather antiquated and our whole approach needed to change.

No-one really likes change, and some older members of the family were so set in their ways, but progress was needed.

Times change and we had to change with the times.

Simmsburgh Castle needed a 'new broom,' so to speak, to give the castle a breath of fresh air and I have to admit, the castle was in need of a good 'airing.'

It was so good to see the old place gradually, being brought back to its former glory, full of hustle and bustle.

My grandmother remarked that such a grand

old place deserved to have lots of people

loving, laughing and living in it.

CHAPTER FOUR

As my time in London was coming to an end,

my father and I decided to spend a whole

week together. Our retrospective work in

London, regarding the family affairs, and

castle, was 'done and dusted.'

It was wonderful to be able to relax for a time

in my father's company and just chat. We

had both agreed that he would look after our

affairs in London and live in the townhouse,

and I would be based at the castle looking

after all things required in the running of both the family and the estate.

One day, over lunch, my father and I talked on many subjects ranging from the castle, the estate, world affairs, London, to the state of affairs in the United Kingdom. My father remarked, in a rather sober manner, that the world, as we knew it, would soon come tumbling down around our ears; however, and thank heaven for it, he had both the wisdom and foresight, which enabled him to, not only to make the castle secure but the estate and all the family's possessions, too. Every eventuality that we could perceive was put into action and, because of my father's regular and attentive 'sittings' in the House of Lords, it enabled him to see, clearly, through all the red tape and maze of information.

After a while, the conversation turned to my mother. My father and I had never really talked about her before. We laughed at great length as he told me about her in the greatest

of detail.

He said, rather wistfully, 'I may have lost your

mother but I have you, a loving son in her

place.'

Asking my father why he never remarried, he replied, sadly, 'Once you've had the best, nothing else will do.'

Over the coming week, my father and I enjoyed each other's company very much, we wined and dined together every night, and took in a variety of shows, it was a break from the normal humdrum of life. Various friends and family came to visit us; it was nice to relax and spend time with them as well.

On the last day, before I was to return to Simmsburgh Castle, my father and I went to see my paternal grandmother who was residing at The Royale Bettington Hotel. It was at this meeting that I found out more details about myself, about my younger self. I had always had a lot of unanswered questions. My grandmother and father, between them, filled in all the gaps in my life story. It was a most informative meeting and made me feel more content about my life, and myself.

Eventually, plans had to be made for my return home.

Arrangements were made for a chauffeur driven car to pick me up from the townhouse and deliver me back to Simmsburgh with just

half a dozen stops along our way.

Gilbert, the chauffeur, we were told, was an

excellent and safe driver, so I decided that he

would be retained within the family's employ

at the castle.

I instructed him to drive along at a steady

pace, as I was in no great hurry to get back.

During the journey, Gilbert and I found we had a certain rapport, which in our circumstances, I suppose, was more than a little unusual and, over the years we eventually developed a good working relationship; Gilbert kept me informed of things that went on among the castle staff, and also kept me abreast of the 'goings on' around and about the estate and surrounding villages.

As we drove through the cities, towns and villages I enjoyed taking in all the sights. It was a rare thing for people to see a motor car, so many of them stopped and stared as we drove by, some of the children even waved to us, it was a pleasant drive as there was little traffic on the roads: occasionally I took a turn at the wheel, to give Gilbert a break. I did so love driving the car, although on formal occasions, it had to be a chauffeur in the driving seat.

The last stop on the way to the castle was always the Coaching Inn at Tinford which was indeed quite comfortable and well equipped to fulfil all my needs.

On journeys to and fro, I would always stop

for lunch there, and as I kept a room

permanently rented, it felt like a home away

from home, plus the fact that no-one

recognised me for who I was.

After spending the night at the inn, Gilbert would drive us on to the castle the following morning.

CHAPTER FIVE

I awoke at seven a.m. the following morning and an unusual feeling came over me. As I dressed to go down for breakfast, there was an air of gloom. The long, expected, financial crisis had hit the country. It was reported in all of the newspapers, and was the only subject of conversation in the breakfast room and I could see panic and fear in the faces around me.

My father and I had anticipated this crisis and had put plans in reserve for the castle and the family, these would now be acted upon and put swiftly into motion.

Gilbert was up at the crack of dawn. He had read the papers and like a good chap had already made hasty preparations to get me to the castle in haste. He knew instinctively that I would not want to hang around with the situation being as it was. Before leaving the Coaching Inn, I would bring my account up to date and also pay a further twelve months in advance.

We did not leave at the time we had anticipated as there was such a flurry of activity.

The Inn was used by a variety of businessmen toing and froing from London, and I could see the sheer panic in their faces. My father's prophetic words would come true - greed would get them every time.

By the time we left the Coaching Inn, it was ten thirty and we hurriedly made our way on to the castle. Gilbert, God bless him, did not hang about.

On our arrival at the castle, we drove through the gate, under the archway, up the drive and pulled up at the front of the castle where we were met by the senior members of staff.

As one of the staff escorted me to the Long

Room, there was a certain buzz about the

place. A project, code named 'Scarlet', had

immediately been set into motion and every

member of staff knew exactly what they had

to do in the circumstances. Initially, I

remained at the castle and kept in close

contact with my father in London. Amongst

the gloom and doom, there were a lot of 'rich pickings' to be had. My father already had his eye on some investments in the city, and the Co-operative Society wasn't backward in coming forward, taking advantage of the situation. My main job was to keep the castle secure and to make sure that it remained on a firm footing. The castle was to be the anchor place for the project, code named SCARLET. This name would become synonymous in, and around, the financial city. In the past many people in the City had wanted to deal with us, because we gave their companies stability. However, the stock market crash would be long and hard and

many companies and people, would go down

losing everything in the crash. After the initial

shocking news, everything looked so black,

but it wasn't the end of the world, for at

Simmsburgh Castle. It gave us the

opportunity to regroup and reform. The castle

was to be totally reorganised, along with the

estate. Some things, such as administration,

were streamlined in order for the department

to be run more efficiently.

One of the biggest changes made, was that

we changed our bankers.

During the crisis, the Simmington Co - operative Society bought a bank, which had found itself in financial distress.

The Co-operative poured money into the system, to make it secure. The castle and the estate, now, with everyone's full agreement, used this bank and all its available resources and facilities.

CHAPTER SIX

Things moved at a furious rate and took a

good nine months for the crises to bottom out

and stabilise, many firms were on the edge of

bankruptcy and thousands of people lost their

jobs. Governments all over the world

organised emergency and special measures

to cope with the financial crisis, but it took

years to turn things completely around and

there were many hardships.

Having predicted the financial crash, my

father had set up a holding company. This

holding company would take care of the various family businesses, from 'all under one roof' as it were, although various individual family members had their own, separate, investment portfolios.

Although we were somewhat flush with money, my father and I agreed to take a cautious approach. We did not rush to go - 'where angels feared to tread.'

So many people had been caught up in the happy go lucky, wild times of the '20's and had spent money as if it were 'going out of fashion.'

Simmington Holding Company, owned by my family, had managed to buy up a number of companies, on the cheap, and in due course, cleared all their debt.

Firms that produced or did similar goods or other things, such as textile mills, were merged, making them into one larger more efficient company. Reducing management structure, and streamlining administration, retrospectively making the businesses more stable, railways, coal mines, ironworks, shops and even a bank, they were all bought and re-organised. So many companies had, in their past histories, just been badly managed and, in many cases, all they needed was a complete overhaul and new management structures installed.

There were new rights for workers, from pensions to sick pay, salaries and even a forty five hour working week was introduced. All workers had fresh terms and conditions. Trade Unions were formed to enable negotiations to be made more effective and efficient; however, although the Simmington Holding Company always maintained a good working relationship with the unions, it still took three long years, together with lots of hard work to complete negotiations and to bring the new plans to their fruition and get

the job done.

In due course, my father would get his

revenge on the people in the City who had

out-maneuvered him five years earlier. He

was back at the top of his game with a fresh

glint in his eye, a fresh spring in his step, and

was beginning to enjoy life to the full again.

Many of the people who had been involved

had fallen from grace.

In the long run, it wasn't a bed of roses for the

public in general, but, by 1932, the recovery,

although slow, had begun to be noticed in earnest.

While my father remained in London, new opportunities arose for us, and the family. We took full advantage of all the new methods and new technologies.

At the castle we had gas, electricity and running water installed in the main rooms, along with updated toilet facilities and a completely new sewerage system was installed.

While the castle was being brought into the twentieth century, the old building was turned upside down, along with our lives, but, then again, the whole world had been turned

upside down, but, by this time, we were able,

thankfully, to look toward the future.

CHAPTER SEVEN

Christmas 1933 was approaching and it had already been agreed that this was the time of year that all the family should gather together in one place namely the castle. It had become too easy, due to the modern ways of life, for people to drift apart. From now on, all the family would gather together every year.

It became a family tradition and long may it continue to be so, and it did not go the way of so many plans of the past, which had fallen, sadly, by the wayside. A lot of things, in years gone past, had fallen by the wayside.

The family decided to put on a full, and jolly good show. Heaven knows, there were so many people needing work. The servants, since the war, had been reduced, but the Co-operative Society had been brought in to help them out.

A novel idea came to mind (I don't remember exactly who came up with it) to employ an Event's Manager.

After a telephone conversation with my father, he told me that he knew just the chap for the job, Walter Forton who was about to retire from the Grenadiers, and was at that moment a Garrison Sergeant Major with the Welsh Guards. My father's instincts were always right, and we knew immediately that Walter was just the right person and would do a splendid job. From now on he took charge of all castle events, from garden parties to weddings, he organised them all, with the expected, military precision.

The first major test for Walter would be that Christmas.

Walter commandeered a suite of rooms at the rear of the castle, heaven knows, there were enough of them spare, and made them into

his and other staff offices.

A small group of extra staff were taken on, in

order for Walter's Team to function efficiently,

however, when a major event was to take

place, even more staff were drafted in from

elsewhere.

Although that particular Christmas would be

somewhat slightly subdued, it would be built

on in future years.

Christmas trees would come from the estate

forest, along with most of the food, especially

turkeys, of which we had the best pick, - but it

did seem strange to be planning Christmas in summertime.

True to form, the castle ran like clockwork and all the guests' invitations were duly dispatched, and all staff put on standby. The main guest on our invitation list was the Dowager of Stonehaven Manor, third cousin to my wife, Gertrude. Sadly, as it turned out, all her family would be away for the festive season, busy on official duties of state leaving her on her own.

The Dowager was so grateful for the invitation, that in her reply, she invited Gertrude and I for a short visit before the holiday season began, which we did, and had a very pleasant time over the following three weeks.

Finally, the big day arrived, Christmas Day, from breakfast to dinner, the whole castle was just filled with hustle and bustle and seasonal goodwill.

Retreating to the library with my father, for a short respite from the jollifications, I could see by his demeanor that it was just what 'the doctor ordered' for him. Sadly, he had never really celebrated a single Christmas since my mother had passed away, but this year, he drew great comfort from being involved in all things Christmas. We chatted for a while,

once again quietly enjoying each other's

company, before rejoining the family and the

rest of the Christmas festivities.

CHAPTER EIGHT

When the Christmas Season was over, our guests left for their own homes, and the castle returned to normal. Our lives went on, but things were not well with the world, worrying stories were coming out of Germany, and I was reminded of my father's remarks after the Great War when he said - 'this is not the end of it, mark my words, there will be another war.'

At the castle, many things, such as the family heirlooms and treasures were not taken out of the safety of the vault when the Great War had ended. It was decided to leave all the valuables in storage.

Above stairs in the castle, we were minimalistic in our approach and coped with what we had. No new furniture, paintings or items of luxury would be bought for the foreseeable future.

However, with an eye on the happenings in Europe, we did spend money on the defence of the castle, such as air raid shelters. This must have seemed, at the time, pessimistic to say the least, but father was convinced that another war was inevitable, that it would be another world conflict, and he decided that

Simmsburgh Castle would be well prepared.

Along with the majority of the population,

many of the politicians could not, and would

not, believe there would be another war, they

thought it could be averted, but wiser people,

seeing what was happening in Germany,

feared the worst.

Neither my father nor I relished the thought of

another conflict, but we agreed with the

sentiment of the times, the United Kingdom,

along with the rest of the world, was slowly

sleepwalking towards a second world war.

As I wanted to check on how things were on

the estate, I told Gilbert, my chauffeur, to

bring the car 'round to the front of the castle

and had George, my valet, come along as

well. As we drove off my thoughts were, that if

war did eventually come, then the castle

could not be in better hands, with my wife

Gertrude at the helm.

Gilbert drove me straight to Florence Hill,

from where I could survey the surrounding

estate. It was a chance for Gilbert and I to

talk informally, as we were 'not on parade' as

it were.

Mildred, who was in charge of the kitchens,

had packed a splendid food hamper for us,

so, before eating, Gilbert and I and my Old

English sheepdog, Lassie, went for a good brisk walk to stretch our legs, leaving George to organise the spreading out of the picnic in all its splendour. When we returned the three of us tucked in, relaxing in each other's company and keeping the conversation, though general, quite informal.

We surveyed the splendid, panoramic view, from arable flat lands on our left, to the estuary way over to our right. It was an awesome sight to see, as one could also take in all the surrounding villages as well. I did so enjoy explaining to Gilbert and my valet all aspects of the running of the estate and from this vantage point they could see precisely what I was talking about.

It was inevitable that we became closely acquainted, for, when we were alone, Gilbert and George were more like friends than servants. We remained on Florence Hill for most of the day, for it was a rare, but welcome experience and an escape for all three of us. We talked about the future and what it held in store for us. Florence Hill was such a quiet and peaceful spot and when I was there, I felt free to think my own thoughts with no interruptions.

Times do change and as I kept thinking, we all must change with the times, the world around us was changing, and in many cases, those changes were definitely not for the better.

I advised both Gilbert and George, to move their families from London and settle them in one of the surrounding villages, (something

which they eventually did.)

 We spent the most wonderful few hours on

Florence Hill on that beautiful spot, but it did

feel rather like the 'last of the summer wine.'

The castle and the estate looked glorious and

it positively glistened, spread out before us in

the splendid, afternoon sun. Time flew by

and I never did get to check on the estate as

I'd intended, I remarked to my companions

that I would have to make those checks

another day.

CHAPTER NINE

Returning to the castle, I found that Gertrude had arranged, with cook, the most delicious menu for dinner that evening, all the family were to join us, as always, it was so good to spend time with them, enjoying their company and being totally relaxed. After dinner, I spent the rest of the evening, playing a little snooker in the games room and catching up on my reading in the library. It was the perfect end to a perfectly splendid day. Sometimes one never realises just what one has, even when it's staring you in the face, for it can be rather lonely, sometimes, at the top. Sometimes a sense of duty can be a burden, 'noblesse oblige', and all that that entails. But I had the good sense to keep things in their right and proper place and I always kept myself well occupied on those rare occasions. My attention often wondered with my thoughts turning to the future and what was in store for our family fortunes. At least, by that time the world's economy had stabilized and the castle was on a firm footing. All the estates had, by now, been whipped into pretty good shape. We had modernized, slowly but surely, moving forward and not looking back. The day came around for me to make that tour of the estate which I had left uncompleted some weeks before. Gilbert got the car ready, but this time, I did not take my valet, George. We set off after breakfast, and as we drove, we took in the beautiful vista, once again, from the top of Florence Hill, but this time there was no stopping for a picnic. We made our way to St James,' the family church, which had been built centuries earlier. All my ancestors were buried there, even extended family members. St James' was the Parish Church of not only the market town

of Simmsford, but also that of the castle and

surrounding estate.

Because of the nature of the church, the

cemetery and crematorium were larger than

was usual, covering three hundred acres.

There were smaller cemeteries dotted about here and there, but St James' was the main one.

As a part of making the estate more secure, a trust fund was set up for the church, into which I donated one million pounds. The same with the cottage hospital, which had grown somewhat over the years. There were no free healthcare and the local people benefited from, and with, the little hospital. Various family members, over time, became presidents, chairmen and held other positions with different trust funds set up for different purposes.   One of the lessons learned in high society was that continuity and stability is everything, and although life moves on and we must move on with it, it was always rather comforting to continue in following some of the old traditions of ages past.

On my drive out, I paid a visit to my solicitor, to make improvements and amendments, to all the trust funds covering a variety of things, all a part of making the castle and estates more secure.

While I was keeping my appointment, Gilbert went for a well-earned break, he walked around the village, telling me later that he'd

been looking at property with a mind to

moving his family out from London as I had

suggested some time before.

From a legal point of view, the castle and the

estate were in 'rude health.' but I still decided

to have a meeting at the bank. The bank had

survived the great depression, and had

recovered quite nicely, it had benefited from

all the reorganisation at the castle and estate,

and also from the many new businesses

which had sprung up around and about.

Expansion, however, was not on the cards, for it was decided to concentrate on what we had Craigsburgh Castle.

Natural growth and the building up of the reserves, was the order of the day.

CHAPTER TEN

After finishing all my business in Simmsford, Gilbert arrived to pick me up and we made our way to my favourite Coaching Inn at Tinford. I had previously left instructions at the castle for my valet to meet me there.

George had arrived well ahead of me and had already unpacked my small suitcase containing a fresh change of clothes. I changed and went down for lunch, where I saw the Dowager of Stonehaven Manor, sitting alone in the dining room, apparently, she was there recuperating after a short illness, she called me over and invited me to join her at her table and we chatted, amiably over our lunch, the main topic of conversation being the renovation and modernization of our homes, for the Dowager had been doing the same at Stonehaven Manor as I was at Simmsburgh Castle. When the Dowager found herself a widow, it had hit her hard, but her saving grace was Stonehaven Manor which had stood empty for some seventy years, or so.

Over time, the Dowager would breathe new life into the grand manor.

In a snap decision, I decided to spend an extra couple of days in the company of this most loved and respected relative of my wife's, talking over old times and of how her son, the Duke of Garswoodshire, was managing his estate at Castle Craigsburgh As always, all good things come to an end and we had to say goodbye, but we knew we would see each other again, as usual, at Easter, at Stonehaven Manor.

It was rare for me to have a little 'down time' as most of it I seemed to be always on the go, toing and froing, from one place to another, or one meeting to another. One of the many

obligations of the family, each year was that

Simmsburgh Castle would host the County

Fair within its grounds, it was my wish that

this should continue to be the tradition.

The family usually had its own marque, from

which some members of the family would

'meet and greet', and present prizes to the

winners of the various competitions held.

There were competitions involving the

children, such as the three-legged races, the

egg and spoon race and the sack race. There

were also competitions for produce grown on

the home farms, best animals in show, flower

arrangements and even for the best, local, Brass Band.

Easter was before the date of the County Fair, so we arrived at Stonehaven Manor, as scheduled. It was always a pleasure to see the Dowager, she so loved being the centre of attention and Gertrude spoiled her, shamefully. The staff at the Manor put on a really good show, we 'hunted' for Easter Eggs and charged madly around the grounds taking part in the paper chases, even the surrounding Manor gardens put on a splendid show, with their colourful flower beds, looking wonderful on that bright, spring day.

I took the opportunity, while we were there, to take a closer look around the house, to see if there was anything new that I could learn from the gardens, kitchens and home farms, all the intricacies that made Stonehaven function successfully.   Everything was interlinked and the house and estate ran like clockwork which was exactly as I expected, with the Dowager in charge.

While we were all there for the Easter weekend, arrangements were agreed upon and put into place, for both estates to work together. We would share ideas and a land/lease agreement was made. There were many new ways of doing things and the

Dowager, being an American, was more open

to new ideas and ways of doing things than

many of the English Aristocracy.

Having a trade agreement between the two

estates was most useful and much was

learned. Even the Duke of Garswoodshire

and my father were in on the plans. One of

the main things that came from the said

agreement were the new working conditions

for all staff in the castle, at the manor house

and, on the estate, in the way of a pension

fund, from which the members would benefit,

and to which both castle and staff would

contribute.

CHAPTER ELEVEN

Returning to the castle, after that Easter

weekend with the Dowger at her mansion,

was such a strange experience. I looked at

Simmsburgh with a new pair of eyes.

From the glory days, through the Great War,

things had changed and there was a whole

different mood in the country.

Simmsburgh Castle had survived, unlike

many other estates.

I felt that I needed to take some time out for

myself, so I made my excuses, said I was ill,

and took some time out and moved into a local cottage.

I took Gilbert with me, a cook and a maid, they ran the house while I recovered.

The family doctor called in once a week, to check on me. But, I knew that all I needed was rest, it had been hard work getting the castle back on its feet. All the necessary people were in place to run the castle and the estate in my absence

Gilbert stayed with me all the time, but my 'cottage servants' were rotated. It was nice to get closer acquainted with the staff, after all, without them, basically, the castle could not function at all.

During this time both Gilbert and I became firm friends. We shared stories - from upstairs and downstairs - some of which were quite revealing. There were indeed many stories about the castle and our family, as it had such a rich and varied history.

It had always been a frightening thought for me that this was in my inheritance, that I was, in actual fact, in charge of it all. But I knew, as I had always known, that it could not be done by one person alone. The castle had, and would always need good, loyal staff.

Education would be the way forward, new ways of doing things must come to the fore, but some of the old traditions would be upheld. I fully understood that the world was changing and we must change with the times. Walking leisurely through the local village was an absolutely fabulous experience, it opened my eyes.

Living in the castle was like living in a fish bowl but walking around the village streets I saw how others, less fortunate, really lived. From the shops, parks, and gardens and the different houses those people lived in.

While resting in the drawing room after one of these walks, Gilbert and I had a serious heart to heart discussion, about all manner of things, his future, my future, the future of the castle.

As much as I loved Simmsburgh and the estate, I knew that occasionally, whatever was happening at the castle, in the family or the world at large, I would have to leave time for just myself and Gertrude.

But while I had this opportunity at the cottage, I intended to make the most of it, spending time reading, walking, or just relaxing, in fact - time just for myself.

To repeat something Gilbert said to me as we

talked

'The castle will be there when you are not, the

castle will live on forever.

THE END

In memory of my dear father

George Naylor

13th February 1937 - 19th April 2020

Reunited with my mother

Dorothy Anne Naylor

30th July 1941 - 13 May 2015

The best parents a son could ever have

Paul Naylor

Books in Series

Stonehaven Manor

Stonehaven Manor the war years

Stonehaven Manor post war years

Stonehaven Manor the Dowager

Me Owd Fettler

Yew Tree Farm

Printed in Great Britain
by Amazon